To Neil

C000178932

THE MASTER

A Journey of Meaning and Purpose to Define Your Mindset

How to develop your mindset to be the best version of you.

Keep on writing
Dreams are there
for the dreamers

Paul

Paul Corke

First Published by AuthorHouse in 2008 under the name The Master: Be Your Personal Best

This version published 2018 by Amazon The Master: A Journey of Meaning & Purpose to Define Your Mindset.

A CIP catalogue record for this book is available from the British Library.

ISBN 9781717957412

Special thanks go to Rachel Corke for review and Lee Deakin for cover design.

About the Author...

Paul Corke is an Author, Leadership Thinker, Mindset Coach, Speaker & Facilitator specialising in mindset, leadership and organisational development. Paul has extensively researched what makes people successful and has published a number of successful books on mindset.

Paul is the Founder of an innovative leadership consultancy, Leadership Architecture. Paul uses his business, academic and sports' experience, along with his leadership thinking, to help organisations create leaders who are resilient and agile, ready to move with the ever-demanding change and uncertainty we face in the modern world. Paul ensures organisations have the right leadership architecture in place to future- proof leaders in alignment with business strategy.

Also, by Paul Corke...

Reframe Your Mindset: Redefine Your Success

The New Positive Thinking: In Search of a Positive World

For my beautiful daughter India, you are my inspiration. Always be your personal best, I love you.

For all genuine people

In life, we all have a choice, choose wisely my Fandango

THE MASTER
A Journey of Meaning and Purpose

"Though we travel the world over to find the beautiful, we must carry it with us or we find it not."

- Ralph Waldo Emerson

Content

'Without leaving my house, I know the whole universe.' - Lao-Tsu

LOOK TO THIS DAY
For it is life, the very Life of Life,
In its brief course lie all the Varieties
and
Realities of your existence;
The Bliss of Growth
The Glory of Action
The Splendor of Beauty
For Yesterday is but a Dream,
And Tomorrow is only a Vision;
But Today well lived makes every
Yesterday a Dream of Happiness
And every Tomorrow a Vision of Hope.
Look well, therefore, to This Day!

- From the Sanskrit

THE MASTER

'Before I had studied Zen I saw mountains as mountains, waters as waters. When I learned something of Zen, the mountains were no longer mountains, waters no longer waters. But now that I understand Zen, I am at peace with myself, seeing mountains once again as mountains, waters as waters.' - Ch'ing-yuan

PROLOGUE

There is a misty sky stretching towards the morning sun. To the right sits an old temple, perched upon the mountainside, with grass cliffs surrounding from both sides. A river runs through the landscape, flowing towards the sea, and out unto the vibrant setting sun. On both sides of the river stand two tall windmills with their sales blowing gently from the wind, moving in different directions. Hidden lie remains of old ways awaiting re-birth that are deeply embedded upon the landscape. Fallen like memories, footprints upon the mind of the world.

I have walked upon many winding steps until I reach a door....

'So, where do we begin?'

'*Master will you teach me*?'

'What would you have me teach that you do not already know?'

'*O Master you are so wise, I would like to know about love and life, the mystery and the secret, the essence and the realm. I desire illumination and enlightenment in learning all there is to know.*'

'Is knowledge power then? For is it not ignorance you seek if your search is for happiness because, young one, ignorance is bliss? But I guess you would never settle for a life of not knowing and being free to observe with silence. Young fool that wants to know and old fool that thinks he knows. Same difference but different times of life.'

'*Do we share the same journey Master?*'

'Tie two birds together and although they have four wings they cannot fly.'

'*So, my path awaits me with each step I take and each footprint I make upon this tale of living?*'

'Each path is separate in this world alone, alive, and we experience everything but take nothing with us. We walk the threads of fate and shape our destiny in destiny's garden. Most walk the path chosen but the few through enlightenment make their own path through the power of their choices.'

'Master you are so wise; you are my inspiration.'

'Be your own inspiration and be inspired by being present young one. For who am I to lecture? For I know I know nothing at all and I awake each day with a blank mind ready for the day's lesson. Let's walk upon this balcony to look upon the river where the phoenix fly's high and let our minds wander free with the flowing of running water. As with each breath we take we become one with the nature of our time, we become an illusion of the conscious mind. Yes, we are like fools, you and me, who dare to believe we exist to find meaning for our existence when we are already born with meaning, purpose and universal cause. **Each one of us born unique, special and part of the pattern of the universe**. Each of us hidden from the truth and searching for what we feel is missing. So, my young Fandango where would you like to fly this night?'

'Please Master will you tell me the seven noble truths of human dynamics, the path and the way, the love and the life, the man and his wife, the forwards and backwards, the splendor and the strife.'

'Yes, we shall travel along the path and the way of the seven noble truths and discover humanity's sorrow and delight, but first let's look to the sky.'

The door opens upon the glorious misty sky…

'Where do we begin?'

'Tell me what you see?'

'A glorious coloured sky as the sun sets that fills me with wonder'

'What do you feel?'

'A feeling of exhilaration in the present moment when observing all around me. I hold fascination for my lot and all things in life. I feel like I have been here before in another life that I can feel the whole of humanity's sorrow and the beauty of a thousand tales that created a thousand worlds. I feel the well of sadness with the exhilaration of joy for the

power in one life is enough to create a thousand worlds.'

'What do you smell?'

'The cinders of a burning fire, the crispness of the grass and the scent of the wildflowers, I smell life all around like a force that binds everything together.'

'What do you taste?'

'I taste the freshness of life and cry out for more; I lust for understanding and I search for the heart's content.'

'What do you hear?'

'The beating of my heart in answer, the breeze upon my face, the movement of the windmills playing a harmony across the sky that makes one stand with inspiration and stillness, alone with all of humanity's questions etched across the fading sky.'

'And what if everything you saw, tasted, felt, heard and smelt was an illusion of your mind. What if every experience was a fabrication and you were yet to awaken to the truth.'

'No that cannot be my Master for everything I see, I touch, I taste, I feel, I hear, I smell is who I am and the world I live in. It is what we are. Why transcend the essence of our life and the realm of living for it is everything? The freedom to enjoy the vastness of life to be and become all one can be.'

'My young fool, what more purpose can there be for a universe than for an observer to observe it exists. For if you did not and there was no observation then what can possibly ever exist?'

'Master no, there has to be more...for every experience, everything I see, and I feel there is perfection all around me in the sadness of humanity and the joy of human life.'

'Life happens, let's now sit together in meditation to stop from the race to become something, or to be someone, and simply watch the sun set. Let's enjoy this moment as the pinnacle of our life in the here and now.'

'Master where do we begin?'

'Patience Fandango, patience, we always start at the end although some would call that a beginning.'

—

'Master am I ready?'

'We are all ready, for where there is a will there is a way.'

*'You ask why I live alone in the mountain forest,
And I smile and am silent until even my soul grows
quiet: It lives in the other world, one that no one
owns. The peach trees blossom. The water flows.'*

- Li Po

What do you really know?
What do your senses tell you?
Where do you really live?

'A university professor visited Zen Master Nan-in to inquire about Zen. But instead of listening to the master, the scholar kept going on and on about his own ideas. After listening for some time, Nan-in served tea. He poured his visitor's cup full, and then kept pouring. The tea flowed over the sides of the cup, filled with the saucer, spilled onto the man's pants and onto the floor.

'Don't you see that the cup is full?' the Professor exploded. 'You can't get any more in.'

'Just so,' replied Nan-in calmly. 'And like this cup, you are full of your own ideas and opinions. How can I show you Zen unless you first empty your cup?'

THE MASTER

'Practice and realization are identical. Because one's present practice is practice in realization, one's initial negotiation of the Way in itself is the whole of original realization.... As it is already realization in practice, realization is endless; as it is practice in realization, practice in beginningless.' - Dogen

Chapter 1 The Brain

Thrown across time with the opening of a book the landscape becomes a blank mirage across the desert awaiting a tale in the making. Bones lay scattered across this landscape in different shapes and sizes, sacramental to the history of life and stories gone untold, until we reach an ancient gold building.

It is Egyptian architecture in nature with visions of animal gods sculpted and drawn. The setting is an island with two giant statues of the God Horus either side of a meridian line leading to a giant blue doorway.

The doorway stands like a vast opening in to the very life of mankind. Artificial lighting mixes with incense which burns to create a mirror of light. Across the walls are giant Egyptian figureheads and golden hieroglyphics as water surrounds to leave a small island. Every part of the building gleams with gold like a newly built alter to life ready for the sacrifice of the day.

The Master opens the door and the apprentice follows, walking through the door three times to get to the other side. There is a feeling we have been here and there before. Deja vu, intuition, spiritual insight, associations, patterns, gut feeling, humanity's sorrow and joy, the essence and the realm.

'What does it mean to be alive my young apprentice?'

'It is a gift my Master that we should make the most of and so we should always try to understand the nature of our virtues and our shortcomings. We should make the most of each day we are alive, that we breathe. '

'Here is the first lesson Fandango...'

The Master draws a picture.

'What is that?'

'A tree?'

'Look again,' he says with laughter.

'A cloud'

'Think with your head - in fact what is inside your head?'

'A brain'

How does a brain relate to life?

'We have to use our brain to function?'

'Really!'

'O*k that was a statement of the obvious, we need to have an open mind, and the brain is where all our reality exists through our conscious thoughts*?'

'What else?'

'The left side of the brain functions more logically and the right more imaginatively?'

'Yes, agreed and dependent upon your preference might depend your outlook on life but there is more.'

'There are three main parts of the brain the thalamus, the neo cortex and the amygdala.

Any visual picture experienced goes straight from the eye to the thalamus where it is interpreted by the brain. The message then goes to the visual cortex where it is giving meaning and purpose. If the meaning is emotional then a signal goes to the amygdala to ensure we make the right emotional response?'

'I see...'

'However, part of the original signal goes straight from the thalamus to amygdala meaning that we respond emotionally before we have time to interpret and add full meaning. It is what is known as the amygdala hijack that we let our emotions rule our lives.'

'Hmmmm and where have your answers come from?'

'What I have learnt in the past....'

'Is this true?'

'What is true? But yes, I am led to believe it is a fact?'

'I see the facts of life that shape your life through experience and what untold boundaries does that present?'

'That I become a condition of my circumstances?'

'Here we have it, the tower of one's mind entrapped in a world of emotional response and conformity. It is time to free your mind and find enlightenment in the freedom of your choices.'

'What does this mean Master?'

'If I say the word '**conditioning**' what does that mean to you?'

'We are already conditioned by every experience that we are programmed to instantly respond without thinking."

'Yes and...?'

We are conditioned by every experience that we can become so set in our ways. In life we continue to live the same life over and over again, doing the same things and making the same decisions.'

'Expand....'

'Well every experience is etched upon your mind likes grooves on a vinyl record that when an experience repeats itself, we don't stop to think we just react.'

'What examples would you give me?'

'Master, I think I understand that perhaps it is like if I am having a bad day then I lose my freedom to stop, think and act for myself. I am programmed to react and to act. In fact, if I am hassled, I can repeat the same destructive behaviour over and over again. I think and act without thinking. The amygdala hijacks my life!'

'Yes, let's expand with a question: After having a great bank holiday weekend and then on the Tuesday the alarm clock goes off first thing in the morning what is the first thought that comes into your mind?'

'O no I've got to go to work, I want to stay in bed.'

'An instant reaction and associative pattern of the brain, the workings etched upon your deeper subconscious, the subterranean landscape of your mind. What then if you awaken and when opening the curtains, you find that it is pouring with rain, what would you and most people think instantly?'

'It's a miserable day.'

'And what do most people then let happen for the rest of the day?'

'They have a miserable day because of the weather. In fact, so much so that a person's mood can be set for the day or even the week.'

'And what if once you had showered and dressed you ran downstairs to find your keys had been moved, what then?'

'I would curse everyone else in the house for moving them as I am late and in a rush.'

'How do you normally find your keys then?'

'When I stop to think I usually find my keys, instead of blaming other people for moving them and running around the house like a lunatic. In most cases they have not been moved I have misplaced them or forgotten where I have left them. '

'Yet in the red mist of your anger you react and blame other people, that is where most people live their lives in a deep red mist, blind to the truth, conditioned in a lot of cases to lose. What a shame few learn and choose the freedom of their own response.'

'I see my Master we are born to win but conditioned to lose.'

'What is the first thing that comes in to your mind when I say the word Machine?'

'Machine gun.'

'What responses could you have given?'

'Many different responses my Master, sewing machine, slot machine, computer as a machine for example.'

'Yet you gave me an instant response because we are all programmed by every experience in life and every experience is etched upon our souls. We live in a perception prison and your perception creates your reality.'

'I see we are programmed to respond which means that we act without thinking, which

*means that we continue to do the same things, which means **If we always do what we have always done we will always get what we have always got** and isn't a definition of insanity **doing the same thing but expecting to get different results**?'*

'If you really want to understand how deep this rabbit hole goes then change the tap heads on your sink, put the hot on the cold and vice versa and see how long it takes you to change beyond your conditioning so that it becomes natural to use the cold or hot tap again. This exercise alone will give you a clear understanding of how deep you're conditioning goes Fandango.'

'Why do we not realize this is so?'

'A number of reasons but two spring to mind, comfort and conformity. What do I mean?'

'That we can become stuck in our comfort zones and it normally takes effort to step out of that zone and we tend to conform with other people to be liked. It takes a lot of effort to stand out and be different'

'Yes, why swim upstream against the current when you can swim the opposite way in numbers and safety?'

'What does this all mean?'

'The fact is we do know but we just don't realise. Our conditioning means we are programmed to act without thinking. Let's use the example of the Mother who screams and shouts at the children for not tidying the room, the doorbell rings and it's the friend. What then happens?'

'She talks to the friend?'

'Not only does she talk to the friend but in most cases, she will change her state to be friendly and civil then once the friend has gone what happens? She finishes the conversation with her friend in a nice way, but she is still screaming at the kids in her head that when she closes the door she starts shouting at the kids again. So, her pattern of thinking has not been interrupted although she demonstrates the freedom of her choices by not screaming at the friend.

'I see Master...'

'Or she stops to think when talking to her friend, breaking her pattern of thinking. Hence that when she returns back to the kids the screaming stops because she has realised her behaviour is not appropriate and the pattern has been broken. The point is the Mother has the freedom to choose her response in any situation and quite obviously makes this point by not continuing to scream and shout at her friend.'

'So, we have the freedom to choose our response?'

'Yes, but the rabbit hole goes deeper than purely having the emotional intelligence to choose your response. **I am talking about the ultimate intelligence to choose who you want to be at any time.** This is not the rational versus the emotional but the psychological choice to programme yourself to be who you want to be, to react how you want to respond, and to be your most natural self - the person you were born to be.'

'How?'

'Because if you realise you are conditioned then you have the freedom to stop and not only choose your response but to create the internal landscape of your mind. How? Well you stop and take a look at your life and decide who you want to be, what you want and where you want to go. You also analyse how you have previously been conditioned and re-condition yourself to be who you want to be - you create the internal landscape of your mind.'

'So, in fact I can decide and choose my life?'

'You have the freedom to choose who you want to be when you want to be at any given time – that is psychological intelligence. You can create yourself and you can choose to be the best version of you every day. Who do you choose to be today?'

'All that we are is the result of what we have thought. The mind is everything. What we think, we become.'
- Buddha

Who do you want to be?
What do you want?
Where are you going?

'You know the moment you wake up, have you ever noticed, by the way, that you don't know who you are, and you wake up and you don't know who you are. Have you ever noticed how you look around the room to orient yourself, and what is really surprising is when you see the person next to you and for that split moment you don't know who they are? I think we should contemplate that a lot. We spend the next moments before you get out of bed re-orientating, re-bonding with an identity that for a moment we didn't even have, and the identity is that (thing) we start to form when we take a look at the person next to us.

And then we get up, we start searching our bodies....and then we get up and we go to the latrine and on the way, we look at ourselves. Why do we do that? Why do you stare at yourself? Because you are trying to remember who you are. It is still a mystery. 'But if you have to remember who you are and remember the parameters of your acceptance and the fence of your doubt, if you have to go through the ritual every single day to remember who you are, what are the chances that your day is going to turn out unique? Very slim indeed. But what if .... before you tried to remember who you were that you remembered what you wanted to be, and maybe that came first before you saw your mate, before you clawed yourself, before you staggered out of bed, scared the cat and saw yourself in the mirror. Before you did all of that you remembered something.

Before I bond ritual of my neuronet, I am going to create a day that is astounding, that will add to my neuronet, that will add to the experience of my life, *and you create your day - create your day.*

In that moment, you are not yet who you are is the most sublime moment in which in that moment you see the extraordinary, you can expect and accept the unordinary, you can accept a pay raise today. If you become yourself, your expectation of a pay raise greatly diminishes. You and I both know that. But in this state of non-conclusiveness about your identity, you can create anyway.

So, I tell my students, before you get up and remember who you are, create your day. Then after you create your day, your routine will change. You will be a slightly different person staring at the urinal, looking in the mirror. There will be something different about you, and that will be a wonderful thing.'

- Ramtha Create Your Day - An Invitation to Open Your Mind

THE MASTER

'The body is the bodhi (tree of knowledge)
The mind is a bright mirror in a stand;
Take care to wipe it all the time
And allow no dust to cling.'
- Shin Xiu's Poem Traditional

Chapter 2 The Mirror

Down that rabbit whole we find ourselves in a library high above the gallery, books fill the room across the walls from known history. A musty smell lingers in the air with an array of knowledge scattered across the room. A large rug covers the wooden floor woven with many a thread. There are more doors yet to be opened that offer one the opportunity to explore the next reality or to leave one bound to this one. The reality chosen normally mirrors the landscape of our mind. For we are what we think and what we think becomes our conditioning and so our life.

'So, my Fandango what do you see before you?'

'A Mirror.'

'Look beyond and tell me what you see in the mirror?'

'My Reflection looking back at me.'

'Tell me more?'

'I see myself; I am looking at my face and the clothes that I wear, and I see your reflection too staring at mine.'

'What else do you see?'

'The library behind my reflection and the many doors closed. There are many books of numerous sizes and shapes with stories, facts and fiction enthralled.'

'What don't you see?'

'Master what do you mean?'

'What don't you see?'

'I don't see lots of different things...what do you mean?'

'So, what do you see?'

'I have already explained, I don't understand....'

'You see what you expect to see and miss everything else in the detail. When looking in the mirror most people describe only what they see when there is so much more in how you feel, what you think, what you smell and can taste. In fact, the whole experience of looking at yourself in the mirror is forgotten based on what you can see, how you see yourself and what you are looking for.'

The Master takes his flute and cracks the mirror, the glass breaks into many different parts offering distorted pictures in reflection.

'Master that brings bad luck...'

'All part of your conditioning I make my own luck, what do you see now?'

'A broken mirror.'

'What do you think of that mirror?'

'Well it's broke so it has no use any more as the reflection it gives is not perfect.'

'So, is that how you see your own reflection?'

'Sorry Master I don't mean my reflection is perfect - I am not that vain.'

'I ask you now what you see in the broken mirror?'

'I see many images of myself, my master and the library....in fact the images fascinate me.'

'Yes, my young one, so now you have passed by the limitations of what you expect to see to be able to see? And there is so much more? What is my point Fandango?'

'That there are many ways to see different things in life and that what we see is not always what is there or perhaps we only see what we are looking for?'

'Yes, all of those things and more. The mirror once broken does not fit with the way we want our world to be, for we are attuned to our own ideal forms that exist through our conditioning. We expect a mirror to reflect and not to be broken. Most people never see past their own reflection no matter what else is in the room when looking in the mirror.'

'I see how in the past I have missed the moment because I have not stopped to truly experience that moment, and didn't a famous person say that if you don't stop and take a

27

*look around once and a while you might
miss everything.'*

'And my next point, a normal mirror always
gives you a perfect reflection although you
might not like what you see.'

*'Although what we see in the mirror is always
back to front, so we never really see ourselves
in the mirror like others see us.'*

'How true, however, the reflection is perfect
so why do we not see ourselves like that?'

*'I see myself as a condition of my
circumstances in comparison to society and in
the past, I have counted the value of my life
against what other people have.'*

'And what does it matter what other people
have or possess if you don't have or possess
yourself?'

*'Master to have myself I therefore need to
know myself.'*

'Yes, the point is how do we see ourselves or
in this case what we can find out that other
people know about us. Like with the mirror
we see only what we expect to see or want to

see, so how self-aware are we as individuals and as a collective society? And what do I mean by self-awareness?'

'To be self-aware would be to have insight in to who I am as a person and the effect I have on other people and my surroundings.'

'If psychological intelligence is realising, we can choose to be who we want to be when we want to be at any given time **the next step is having self-awareness to realise who we are now** so we can make the changes and re-condition the landscape of our mind. In so doing it is essential to understand the impact we will have on other people and our surroundings in making those changes.'

'How do we make those changes?'

'By being true to oneself and the vision of who or how one wants to be, **however it is important to remember the mirror as it grasps nothing, it expects nothing, yet it reflects everything.'**

'So, we become our natural self?'

'Yes, and in so doing one acts without effort.'

29

'So where do we start?'

'If one takes the time to consider their ideal self which is the best version of you, which is the natural you, because quite simply if you ask yourself what would the best version of you do in this situation you will always get the most honest, consistent, genuine response. You will be acting with integrity towards yourself and to others.'

'So, my highest hope is my ideal self but once I become my ideal self what next?'

'The ideal self is not an end goal but a way of life - a self one creates every day as the best version of you. Let's rest here my young apprentice before we move to the next plain where the river of life and the test of taking lies. For now, let's simply be.'

'Life isn't about finding yourself. Life is about creating yourself.'
- George Bernard Shaw

When you look at yourself in the mirror who are you?
How have you been conditioned by life?
How can you re-condition the landscape of your mind?

What is the greatest obstacle to experiencing this reality?

Identification with your mind, which causes thought to become compulsive. Not to be able to stop thinking is a dreadful affliction, but we don't realize this because almost everybody is suffering from it, so it is considered normal. This incessant mental noise prevents you from finding that realm of inner stillness that is inseparable from Being.

It also creates a false mind made self that casts a shadow of fear and suffering. We will look at all that in more detail later.

The philosopher Descartes believed that he has found the most fundamental truth when he made the famous statement: 'I think therefore I am.' He had, in fact, given expression to the most basic error: to equate thinking with Being and identity with thinking. The compulsive thinker, which means almost everyone, lives in a state of apparent separateness, in an insanely complex world of continuous problems and conflict, a world that reflects the ever-increasing fragmentation of the mind. Enlightenment is a state of wholeness, of being 'at one' and therefore at peace. At one with life in its manifested aspect, the world, as well as with your deepest self and life unmanifested - at one with Being. Enlightenment is not only the end of suffering and of continuous conflict within and without, but also the end of the dreadful enslavement to incessant thinking. What an incredible liberation this is!

Identification with your mind creates an opaque screen of concepts, labels, images, words, judgments, and definitions that blocks all true relationship. It comes between you and yourself, between you and your fellow man and woman, between you and nature, between you and God. It is this screen of thought that creates the illusion of separateness, the illusion that there is you and a totally separate 'other.' You then forget the essential fact that, underneath the level of physical appearances and separate forms, you are one with all that is. By 'forget,' I mean that you can no longer feel this oneness as self-evident reality. You may believe it to be true, but you no longer know it to be true. A belief may be comforting. Only through your own experience, however, does it become liberating Thinking has become a disease. Disease happens when things get out of balance. For example, there is nothing wrong with cells dividing and multiplying in the body, but when this process continues in disregard of the total organism, cells proliferate, and we have disease.

Note: The mind is a superb instrument if used rightly. Used wrongly, however, it becomes very destructive. To put it more accurately, it is not so much that you use your mind wrongly - you usually don't use it at all. It uses you. This is a disease. You believe that you are your mind. This is the delusion. The instrument has taken over you.

Eckhart Tolle - The Power of Now

THE MASTER

'The monkey is reaching for the moon in the water,
Until death overtakes him, he will never give up.
If he would only let go the branch and disappear into the deep
pool,
The whole world would shine with dazzling clearness.' - Hakuin

Chapter 3 The Cave

The river flows gently through the cave where
a pirate ship rests docked against the wooden
jetty ageless with the tides of history. The sun
shines through the cave on to a platform
where the Master meditates in deep
contemplation, harnessed in the here and now.
No thoughts control his mind, yet his senses
grasp the moment. The visual clearness of the
sky through the cave entrance, the breeze
gentle on his skin, the noise of seagulls at the
edge of the river, the touch of the wooden
floor and the smell of the salt air rising from
the riverbed.

'It is time to take the test.'

'What test Master?'

'I will take you to the Cave of Wonders'

'What will I find in the Cave of Wonders?'

'Everything'

In my excitement, I gather my belongings ready for the test. We walk through caverns into an open swamp, dreary and dark.

It is now night.

Surrounding me are my thoughts as I hear noises in the dark increasing my nervousness. My mind racing with every sound and crack with each step the darkness engulfs my very spirit. I can barely see my Master walking in front of me. *'I can't do this'* my voice echoes with negative conditioning like a demon, *'There is evil ahead'* and all I can feel is evil, the very stench of it, now scared to my bone I feel like I need to vomit. *'You will not be able to pass the test'*, my mind says, *'Why will I not be able to pass the test'*, I ask myself, *'Because you are not good enough you fool.'* Over and over again I hear my own voice, my own negative self-talk as my physiology matches my thought process as my body starts to tense.

It's amazing how if we watch a scary movie when we go to bed how we can then hear every single noise and start to assume there is a mad axe man in the house! How we let our mind race and the power of the subconscious take over.

'Master, wait, I am frightened.'

'What of Fandango?'

'The Dark'

'Rest young one we have finally arrived at the Cave we seek.'

'Where?'

'Between those trees lies wonder more powerful than you can ever possibly imagine.'

'What do I need to take with me?'

'Yourself.'

'I can sense a great evil in the cave, and I am afraid'

'What are you afraid of?'

'I don't know yet as I cannot see what is in the cave.'

Yet my mind is racing, I am scared of the dark, of dying, of being hurt…I place my belongings next to the tree and unleash my sword ready to step in the cave to protect myself.

'You will not need the sword.'

I take it anyway.

I walk inside the cave slowly in fear, trembling, afraid, and scared to my bone. I push past the trees into the cave to find myself in the dark.

This is what I see,

Darkness engulfs me yet my eyes make out faces in the dark, silhouettes, shapes, demons and devils as I thrash out in the dark.

This is what I smell,

A stench of evil rises like thick swirling smog, spiraling upwards from the mud-stricken floor reminding me of a deadly corpse as I start to choke.

This is what I hear,

The noise of the swamp, birds echoing, heavy breathing most likely my own, but what I think is the sound of a beast's shrill breath at a canter.

This is what I taste,

The flavourings of the rumbling swamp in the pit of my stomach as the sweat drips down my forehead on to my lips.

This is what I feel,

Sick to the bone, afraid that I can't go on and that the beast ahead will see me to my end, that I will no longer see the ones I love, that Arcadia must await me as I am now destined to leave this Earth.... crying, scared of dying, scared of loss, afraid to take part and at this precise moment I realise I am the walking dead.

All the thoughts I am thinking creates terror in my experience, which coupled with the combination of my senses heightened with the power of my imagination takes me close to the edge of losing control. The experience becomes deeply embedded upon my mind, conditioned, then I hear the voice of a bird singing which breaks my pattern and then my mind clears to find...

Nothing.

Nothing at all to be afraid off but the imaginations of my own mind that have taken hold of me driving me insane.

Amongst the leaves I find a parchment sealed in the dark, so I take it with me and start to climb into the light.

It is then I realize I have found everything as I read.

'Mind is creative. Conditions, environment and all experiences in life are the result of our habitual, or predominant, mental attitude. The attitude of mind necessarily depends upon what we think. Therefore, the secret of all power, all achievement, and all possession depends upon our method of thinking. This is true because we must 'be' before we can 'do' and we can 'do' only to the extent which we 'are' and what we 'are' depends upon what we 'think'.

There is a world within, a world of thought and feeling and power; of light and life and beauty; and, although invisible, its forces are mighty. The world within is governed by mind. When we discover this world, we shall find a solution for every problem - the cause for every effect. Since the world within is subject to our control, all laws of power and possession are also within our control.

The world without is a reflection of the world within. What appears without is what has been found within. In the world within may be found infinite Wisdom, infinite Power, and infinite Supply of all that is necessary, waiting for unfoldment, development and expression. If we recognise these potentialities in the world within, they will take form in the world without.

The world without reflects the circumstances and the conditions of the consciousness within.' - Charles F Haanel.

And as I climb higher through the branches of the trees like the weight of history and all my conditioning I reach out to the light until I reach the summit and stare in complete awe.

Within me lies everything in the present moment and before me therefore lies the most magnificent landscape of infinite beauty. In happiness, I cry tears of eternal sadness and for the first time I realise I am free in the present moment surrounded by the essence and the realm.

Time stops (But did it ever start?). ....in this moment of inspiration.

Eventually I climb back down to find my Master.

'What have you found?'

'Everything'

'In what way, my young apprentice?'

'I realise that my internal world creates my external world and that the voices in my head I can control. The world within creates the world without.'

'What does the cave represent?'

'The subconscious conditioning of the world and when we realise instead of mindlessly thinking all of the time that we can choose who we want to be, that we can choose the internal landscape, that we can be free of fear

*by having control of one's own mind. What
you take into the cave manifests itself.'*

'What did you take with you Fandango?'

*'Fear created by the endless chatter of my
mind, anxiety based on my past conditioning
and worry about my future state - or lack of
future state through death. I don't want to die'*

'Nobody and no thing want to die yet fear of
death can be worse than death itself. For it is
the fear of being nothing and not existing.
You must let go of this fear for in the end we
all must move from this physical world. You
cannot escape the passing over, but you must
not be paralysed to live this life by fear or it
will pass you by and life lessons will be
missed.'

*'I sense a great shift in humanity's thinking, a
paramount paradigm shift of epic proportions
for we create our own life and we are totally
responsible for the output because it comes
from our input. We can change the world and
we can change our life at any moment in time.
It is a choice and we always have a choice.'*

'Yes, young one it is called a personal
paradigm shift and the opportunity to create

your own internal landscape to create your external universe. The power is yours Fandango. You can have control of your state of mind at any point in time and you can determine your own beliefs, values, attitude, behaviour, response, and therefore your life.'

'What wonder this is, what joy, what freedom I have in this life of free will?'

'We believe that every experience creates the person we are, and it does. We learn and grow from each experience but then we become conditions of our own experience especially when we stop to think about our actions. Our perception has been our reality and we no longer need to be trapped within that perception prison, we are free to decide, free to choose, free to create the life, the person we want to be, the direction and more importantly our fate. **And within our own individual cave, our subterranean landscape lies all the wonder of the world.'**

'Because it goes to the essence of the assumptions of whom you think you are. So, if we think that we are living in a certain kind of world, we behave in a certain kind of way. If we think we are living in a world where human beings are a kind of machine, we're like robots walking around, there may or may not be anything actually happening in there, then

questions like morals and ethics and how we live our lives, and what we think about death and life, those will be very different than if we think the world is an interconnected, alive one.' - Dean Radin

What is your cave filled with?
How can you free your mind?
How can you create your life?

'The Emperor's chief carpenter, Ch'ing, once made a music stand so perfect that all who saw it marvelled. When Lu asked him to reveal the mystery of his art, Ch'ing demurred, saying: 'No mystery, your Highness, though there is something. When I am about to make such a stand, I first reduce my mind to absolute quiet. Three days in this condition and I am oblivious to any reward to be gained. Five days, and I am oblivious to any fame to be acquired. Seven days, and I become unconscious of my four limbs and body. Then, with no thought of the Court in mind, all my skill concentrated, and all disturbing thoughts gone, I go into the forest to search for a suitable tree. It contains the stand in my mind's eye, and then I set to work.'

- Chuang-Tzu

THE MASTER

'How broad, how deep, how high is the level of your acceptance? Because that is what belief is. You can never, ever manifest in your life that which you do not accept. You only manifest that which you accept. So how broad is your acceptance? Is it greater than your doubt? What are the limitations of your acceptance? Is that why you are sick? Is that why you are old? Is that why you are unhappy, because the level of your acceptance is unhappiness? That is all you get, you know. You don't get anything greater.' - Ramtha

Chapter 4 The Wheel

We have travelled to the city where the lights are filled with silver and gold. This hub of humanity is a festival of life surrounded by road upon road and building upon building, infrastructure and architecture. We walk the streets greeting the people who mainly pass by minding their own business, too busy to stop, too busy to think. We enter a square to a festival of life, as music fills the air and movement is everywhere with lives running their course in different directions but interconnecting along the way. Some find meaning, some find despair, some just aren't looking and some just pass you by and you will never notice they ever were.

We enter the Casino to my surprise.

'Master a Casino?'

'Yes, it is important to experience the wheel of life. Here are your chips the hall is yours.'

'But Master that is a lot of money to lose.'

'And there is a lot of money to win.'

'But it is a lottery and I could lose all the money.'

'The chattering of your mind precedes you, how do you ever expect to win?'

'But I can't just think that I'm going to win and then gamble expecting to win because that would mean I am just trying to fool myself and then I could find myself not only with no money but in debt.'

'Why not? Some think life is a lottery, that it is chaos, and life just happens, does it? And therefore, they can't be held accountable for their lot. Some people they say are just 'born lucky' and that's all there is to it. Do you think life is a lottery?'

'No, my Master but gambling is a lottery and I could lose.'

'No, you will lose thinking like that because it is a self-fulfilling prophecy. Your thoughts will create, and your actions will fulfil - **what you believe with a passion you will bring in to your life**, it's as simple as that. **Your expectations become your realities.'**

'But I have just as much chance of losing'

'Yes, you do think like that, so don't play if you can't afford to lose and your life continues to follow with little change, with little growth.'

'Master I am being cautious and in this day and age it is good to play safe.'

'Then at least play, take part in the great circle of life and keep your cards close to your chest but don't not play, don't not take part out of fear, out of the endless chattering of your mind.'

'I see the point of this lesson.'

'Every single moment is a lesson, but right now I ask you to play on the wheel, a simple wager to place your money on red or black...'

'Then I place my money on black.'

The wheel spins and red comes in, the money is lost.

'Master I have lost the money...'

'Good, you have lost, that is fantastic news...'

'But Master I have lost the money how can that be fantastic news?'

'Yes, how does the experience feel, for it is in the something you are taking part, you are part of the universal cycle of being and becoming, the great essence and realm. You need to free your mind from the money and the fear of loss facing life's character-building experiences.'

*'It feels good because I now understand that in this moment lies an experience so precious, I can learn from, for in a moment it is gone ready for me to experience the new moment. **It is my mental state that defines the moment and the meaning I apply to it. Nothing has any meaning other than the meaning I choose** - There is nothing good or bad but thinking makes it so said Shakespeare.'*

'There is something, so we should make the most of the something we have, and we have that something now. What we make of that something is all a matter of choice in the moment, however how many stay present to make that choice and choose the something they most desire?'

I understand that those who lose and then blame their luck, who blame life, who blame everything but themselves are living like lost souls. Living a reactive life that becomes a self-fulfilling prophecy...spiralling out of control into a dark pool of pessimism and negativity. Lacking in self-awareness and accountability.'

'The Dark Side where all negative feelings reside, anger, jealousy, frustration, resentment, obsession, the reactive living in a conditioned world and prison for their mind.'

I see that so many people expect to keep putting their money on black and get a different result in the sense of they keep doing the same things and expect different results with no accountability. Why play if you are scared to lose.'

'That is, it you have to be all in and part of the moment, the life experience.'

*'I feel that a change of mindset is needed, a paradigm shift where **every number is a lucky number and every experience is truly experienced by being present. Some say you can't win all the time but actually when playing you are in the experience of life and winning is all about having the right mindset.**'*

'And as you will find winning will happen more often when you expect it to happen, in fact when you think it does happen in the now - Let me tell you the story of a great runner who when running in the Olympics turned the final corner to be overtaken by his great rival and it that moment he gave in to finish fourth and not even win a medal. In defeat, he admitted that his self-talk became negative because he could not win the gold but what he came to realise is that if he had not given up he would have well beaten his personal best.'

'I understand Master, our self-talk is critical to our success in life. Every thought is a cause, which will ripple in to our life as an effect for good or for bad. The way we think is not only who we are and what we do but it

defines the results that will inevitably happen in our life.'

'And…'

'It is important that we take accountability for our life by saying yes to life and yes to ourselves but importantly that we become conscious of who we are and what we are thinking. That we do not let our inner demons take over our lives, that we do not live a reactive life and that we progress to be part of the universal will.'

'Each of us is the individualisation of the universal will.'

'Yes, life in some respects can be defined by the way you see the world, if you choose to see a dark world filled with negativity then that will be the world that you live in however if you choose to live in the light of a positive world, one filled with the wonder of each moment then that will be one's life experience.'

'It is not only about how you see the world but how the world sees you.'

'This I understand for we are ultimately responsible for what other people experience and how they see us every moment of our lives. Everything we do motivates or de-motivates the people we are with, so great is our responsibility for the thoughts and actions we take. For the life we live, for the code we live by, for the person we choose to be.'

'The internal landscape creates the external landscape Fandango.'

'Yes, it is simple, the input reflects the output and what we believe with passion tends to manifest in our lives.'

'That's why it is so important to consider re-programming the subterranean landscape of your mind.'

'Yes, I see, I need to consider who I want to be, how I want to behave, the character I want to be, what I want to achieve and where I want to go. The great thing is I can model myself on all that I want to, to make me the person and life I want to live. But the key is to believe with passion that I am those things, which the world is conspiring to do me good, that I am unique, that I am whole and perfect.'

**'I see, it is the process of layering your
mind with the chosen conditioning instead
of being a condition of your mind.'**

*'Yes, and to have a constant vision of who you
are, where you are going, what you want,
having a passion and belief in the present
moment that you are all things at one with the
universal will.'*

'Let's test your theory…'

'How?'

'It is simple let's change your thought pattern
and return to the wheel…'

*'I see and believe, for I am lucky in this life, I
win all the time, life conspires to do me good,
the harder I try the luckier I become. I enjoy
every experience in life and learn from it. I
am at one with the universal will. The will
shapes me, and I shape the will, it is my soul's
eventuality.'*

'Then play, young one with the power of your
mind and with psychological intelligence.'

'I bet on red, all of the money this time.'

The wheel spins......with only one possible conclusion.

RED

'Is it luck Fandango?'

'Yes, I have all the luck in the world, take it as Red'

'You have complete power over your life, do you choose to take it or blame the wheel of life for your lot?'

A vivid thought brings the power to paint it; and in proportion to the depth of its source is the force of its projection.

Ralph Waldo Emerson

Are you victim of fate or do you make your own luck?
What is your mental state and mindset?
Do you take risks or play safe?

Three men happened to notice a fourth standing at the crest of a high hill and wondered what he was doing there. The first man said, ' He must have lost his favourite animal,' The second said, 'No, he must be looking for a friend.' The third said, 'He is just enjoying the cool air up there.' The three continued discussing and arguing until they reached the man on the hill. The first greeted the man and said, 'O friend, have you lost your pet animal?' 'No, sir,' answered the man, 'I've not lost any.' The second then asked if the man was looking for his friend, and again the man said no. The third asked if the man was there enjoying the breeze. Again, he said no. Finally, the three said, 'What, then, are you standing here for?'

'I just stand,' said the man.

THE MASTER

*'A monk said to the master, 'Having only recently
arrived at this temple, I seek your guidance,'
The Master asked, 'Have you eaten breakfast?'
'Yes,' replied the monk.
The Master's response was, 'Then go wash your bowl.'
The monk was suddenly enlightened.
What knowledge did the monk attain?' - Traditional*

Chapter 5 The Watchman

We have been driving for hours along a
motorway from the bottom to the top of this
sacred isle. The car moves along the road with
pace as we weave inside and out passing other
cars along the way, all passengers in life with
each destination different. I am driving
without thinking because I am conditioned to
drive, talk, and play with the stereo at the
same time for a mental model of how to drive
is deeply embedded within my subconscious.
I do it without thinking.

'Where are we going?'

*'Master I drive in the direction you requested
I know not the destination.'*

'And what destination would you choose?'

'A lake with mountains and a boat surrounded by nature.'

'And where do you live?'

'In a city'

'I see and what would you choose?'

'I have to live in the city my job is based there.'

'To start you don't have to do anything in this life, you have a choice and what I hear is that your destination is the lake, but your life runs its course in the city. When arriving at the lake what do you find?'

'My natural self.'

'And in the city?'

'My neurotic self I guess conditioned by every experience that I have become a condition of my circumstances. And my perception of what is acceptable to fit in with society means that I am part of my own self- delusion. I have created a prison for my own mind.'

'And when you drive along this road what do you see?'

'I concentrate on the cars in front of me.'

'And when do you stop?'

'When I get to my destination.'

'How many times do you look around you and notice the landscape? How many times do you stop to take a look around you and then go to take a look?'

'I notice places from time to time but never find the time...'

'Everybody is in a rush to go nowhere. If they were going somewhere, they would stop to take a look at that lake and then they would go live by that lake.'

'It is like tunnel vision my Master that we race along the highway in our metal cages, caught in the maelstrom of this life.'

'And do you enjoy life?'

'O yes Master but there always seems to be something missing, something I am searching for, but I can't find it.'

'Perhaps you need to find new ways to look, to hear, to feel, to taste, to smell in the here and now instead of the anxiety of the past and worry of the future.'

'I see my Master; I feel like we were once angels and that we are searching for that part which is missing.'

'Which is?'

'Our wings.'

'Take a left into the mountains high up into the clouds.'

'Where do we go?'

'To see the watchman at the gate.'

'And what will I find there?'

'All in good time.'

We approach a gate like I have never seen before and would only imagine like the gates of heaven. And there stands the watchman at the gate.

'What would you have me do?'

'Go speak to the Watchman.'

I leave the car to meander up the path to the Watchman to find he is watching my every move in the finest detail.

'Good day what would thee ask of the Watchman?'

'What is beyond the gate?'

'Beyond the gate is your subconscious mind.'

'What will be there?'

'Every experience is stored with every emotional response, with every beat of your heart.'

'And why do you watch the gate?'

'Why do you think?'

'To ensure no harm happens to the subterranean realm?'

'I am here to guard against your every thought because every single thought you create will shape your subconscious, and everything the subconscious believes with a passion and emotional content will start to take shape in your life.'

'So, you are my conscious mind?'

'I am the guard against you living your life in a prison and when you let thoughts passed me you shape the external landscape of your life from the internal programming.'

'I see, how have I been doing?'

'How do you think?'

'What can I do?'

'Your emotional responses and conditioning will continue to run your life unless you stop and consider how to control your own mind.'

'You mean like programming a machine?'

'You are the machine and the machine is everywhere.'

'I have a choice to fundamentally choose my reaction and control my emotions?'

'Let me explain how the system works, some would say that it is the great secret against the great known truth.'

'What is the secret and the great known truth?'

'The secret is that your thoughts create your reality and that you can choose your own life through programming your mind, by conditioning yourself to be who you want to be and by believing in this whole heartedly starts to make the thoughts in your mind start to create the reality in your life. It is called the law of attraction.'

'And the truth?'

'The truth is acknowledged and sometimes it is denied but once you have the secret to make it happen with belief in purpose you need will power and a fixation on the destination like it has already happened. Will power creates the absolute.'

'And how do I embrace the secret?'

'This is the first step of psychological intelligence, you consider everything you want to be, every value and belief you want to live by, every experience you want to take, every destination you want to arrive at in this life and you start to re-condition your mind with those values and beliefs to create your attitude and ongoing positive behaviour.'

'How do I do this?

'This first step is Visioning the ideal you or the Super You, the you you most want to be which is normally most likely to be your natural greater self. The best version of you. **This is a process of layering** by repeating each day the exercise of writing down or remembering through repetition and re-affirming the vision.'

'And next?'

'You need to understand the secret, that every negative thought that passes me to your subconscious mind will send negative ripples in your life. You will never be rich if you truly believe that you never will be, you can never be lucky if you think you are not.'

'I understand this from the casino…'

'It is the destructive thoughts that create torment in your life but more importantly it is your everyday thoughts that hold you back. Your mind controls and regulates your body at the same temperature and the same impulse tries to regulate your thoughts to ensure they are consistent with past thoughts and experience. This is called the homeo-static impulse and it maintains the status quo by keeping you in your comfort zone.'

'I have to break the pattern.'

'No, you have to think a new pattern to shape the life you want to lead.'

'So, if I believe I'm not good enough, I never will be'.

'Yes, we never will be, the secret is a combination of the self-talk you use to build your self-esteem and through your self-concept which is benchmarked against your ideal self - the Super You. The skill is the repeating of powerful affirmations to continually programme your mind.'

'So, my expectations become my realities.'

'Yes, you attract into your life that which you are thinking, it is the law of attraction, attitude breeds attitude, behaviour breeds behaviour, you will attract in to your life what you hold in your most dominant thoughts.'

'Thank you, my friend.'

'Thank yourself'

I leave to go back to the car....

*'My Master, I understand in full that **our thoughts create our reality and that the Law of Attraction** means I will attract in to my life what my subconscious dwells upon, and if I don't take control of my mind then I will live life as a condition of my thoughts. I will live in the perception prison.'*

'Let me show you the power of your thoughts through a simple exercise Fandango, close your eyes and imagine the following. In your right hand, you are holding a heavy weight which is holding you down that you can feel the weight dropping to the floor. You feel weak in the arm that it is impossible to lift the weight. In your left arm, you have a balloon and you feel it lifting you up into the sky, it is so light that you can feel your arm being pulled up into the sky. High into the sky as you feel you are going to float away. Remember weight holding you down in your right arm and balloon lifting you up in your left arm. Now open your eyes, what do you see?'

'O Master my right arm nearly touches the floor and my left is reaching for the sky!'

'The power of your subconscious mind in action - that is why it is so important to consider the shaping of your internal mind through every thought that you think.'

'We are here to be creators. We are here to infiltrate space with ideas and mansions of thought. We are here to make something of this life.' - Ramtha

What thoughts are you being conditioned by?
How can you change your thinking?
What do you want in your life?

'The law responds to your thoughts, no matter what they may be. You are the most powerful magnetic in the Universe! You contain a magnetic power within you that is more powerful than anything in this world, and this unfathomable magnetic power is emitted through your thoughts. The law of attraction says like attracts like, and so you think a thought, you are also attracting like thoughts to you. Here are more examples you may have experienced of the law of attraction in your life:

Have you ever started to think about something you were not happy about, and the more you thought about it the worse it seemed? That's because as you think one sustained thought, the law of attraction immediately brings more like thoughts to you. In a matter of minutes, you have gotten so many unhappy thoughts, coming to you that the situation seems to be getting worse. The more you think about it, the more upset you get.

Your life right now is a reflection of your past thoughts. That includes all the great things, and all the things you consider not so great. Since you attract to you what you think about the most, it is easy to see what your dominant thoughts have been on every subject of your life, because that is what you have experienced. Until now! Now you are learning the Secret, and with this knowledge you can change everything.

If you can think about what you want in your mind, and make that your dominant thought, you will bring it in to your life. Through this most powerful law, your thoughts become things in your life. Your thoughts become things!

Thoughts are magnetic, and thoughts have a frequency. As you think, those thoughts are sent out to the Universe, and they magnetically attract all like things that are on the same frequency. Everything sent out returns to the source. And that source is you…

…You have a choice right now. Do you want to believe that it's just the luck of the draw and bad things can happen to you at any time? Do you want to believe that you can be in the wrong place at the wrong time? That you have no control over the circumstances?

Or do you want to believe and know that your life experience is in your hands and that only all good can come into your life because that is the way you think? You have a choice, and whatever you choose to think will become your life experience.'

The Secret - Rhonda Byrne

THE MASTER

Yao-shan was sitting quietly in cross-legged meditation when a monk asked: 'In this immovable position, what are you thinking?'

'Thinking of that which is beyond thinking' said Yao.

'How do you go on thinking that which is beyond thinking?' pressed the monk.

'By not-thinking.' - Zen mondo

Chapter 6 The Will

Outside in the night air, away from the sea I find myself asleep dreaming of an alternative reality. The dream that when you awake you wish you were still dreaming and when you realise the sensations, the feelings, the experience of the dream that have come alive are not real you feel numb.

When you realise that the ultimate control of one's senses within the dream, the feeling of creating one's own reality is the nirvana of the soul then enlightenment in this life occurs. For then we can create the dream in our chosen reality.

'Awaken young one and open your eyes'

'It is so bright, where are we?'

I open my eyes to see a vast red desert and deep blue sky set across the horizon.

'In the desert of lost souls.'

'What is that?'

'What do you see?'

'A desolate landscape, scattered with fallen debris and contusions within the sand.'

'And?'

'The heat rises from the desert as the air constantly reacts to the temperature of the sand and the magnification of the sun.'

'Close your eyes Fandango and create this landscape in your mind.'

'That is easy my Master.'

'Now create the landscape one most desires in detail.'

'I can see a mirage in the desert that starts to form an oasis filled with life. A well stands in

the centre and green vegetation grows surrounded by tents filled with people. They are beautiful people golden in appearance as music plays, animals of different kinds create esoteric noise, and there are smells of food cooking and smoke from the essence of candles. I feel alive as if touched by the atmosphere of warmth and intimacy leaving a taste of life in my mouth for more.'

'And?'

'I can feel water on my face from the refreshing well of life that gives hope to all humanity and the fact the people seem free to create their own destiny, their own fate, their own life through the choices they make.'

'Now open your eyes.'

'Master how can this be?'

'What do you see?'

'The mirage in the desert?'

'Is it not so imaginable that you can create your own internal landscape and in turn that it will create your own experience, has that not been our topic of conversation.'

'But master there was desert and now we stand in the middle of an oasis.'

Perhaps then it is the dream that never was and when life is over another lost soul will never have passed by the desert.

'I understand Master that you have to create your own fate in your mind with 100% certainty that it will happen.'

'Yes, that it has already happened, if you ask the universe for what you want and then believe it with passion the Universal Will will then make it happen.'

'And what is the Universal Will?'

'What is will?'

'My will is to ensure the thoughts I make I then create in my life through the power of my will.'

'Where does that will come from?'

'My will is the will to love because the will to love is to take positive action towards oneself or another.'

'And the opposite?'

'The will to nothing - no will, no action, no change.'

'But why change?'

'Most people live in their comfort zones, the bubble the prison creates in a reactive world of conditioning. The prison for our minds in the desert of the lost souls. The shackles for all human potential. The will to love is of the spirit. It is the will power to create the life we want to live, to sustain the vision of who we want to be. It is our will power that awakens in the morning and re-creates the landscape we desire to ensure that we are not left in the desert of lost souls and that we are not victims of our circumstances.'

'Such as?'

'That we do not waste energy in a negative way by failing to recognize our negative programming, in not recognising the freedom to choose our reaction in any given situation. We do not fail to move ourselves to realise our potential, that we stagnate and grow old and wish 'what if'. Letting go of that negative

energy because there is an abundance of wealth and prosperity that the universe is willing to give if we believe that the universe is conspiring to do us good. It begins with the positive creation of one's values, beliefs, principles, the creation of the Super You and the life you want to live. The person you want to be, the way you want to react, the achievements you want to make, the places you want to visit, and the peace within your soul. Life has no boundaries and the limits of human potential are endless. To follow the creation one needs to have the will power to see it through, to wake every day and think those thoughts, to be self-aware at all times, to take positive action in line with one's highest hope, the vision of the ideal self and the belief in certainty that it will happen, it has happened.'

'So, there are two paths you can take?'

'Yes, the path that leads to no change, to waiting for life to happen, to being a victim of one's circumstances, continuing to react to one's programming so that life happens to you instead of creating one's life. You continue to live in a prison for your mind.'

'The other path?'

*'The path of enlightenment is to wake to this dawn with the salutation of the day because you have the freedom to choose who you want to be when you want to be at any given time, **that we can create our day, our life, our world,** that we have the freedom to choose our reaction, that we can shape the subterranean landscape of our mind to be our ideal self, our natural self, that **we can create our circumstances** instead of being a product of them, that we can attract into our life the things we want the most through trust in life, through the thoughts we make, through the actions we take and through our will to love.'*

'How can I see which road you have taken?

'You will see positive action, an aura of certainty, strength of character, a contented soul that takes consistent action in line with one's vision of the Super You.

'What will I feel?'

'Positive energy that creates more positive energy, attitude breeds attitude, you gravitate into your life the things you think about the most, you attract into your life people and situations based on the way you think.'

'What is it that makes the difference?'

'Who you are being in this life is the difference that makes the difference. You can be who you want to be, you can change your state, you can change your energy at any given to time to create the circumstances you want in your life.'

'Is this then Nirvana for the mind?'

'If you create the vision, think consistent thoughts in line with that vision, take consistent action with belief in certainty that it will happen. Using your will power to ensure that consistency takes place eventually it will become a habit that it will be that deeply embedded in the subconscious that two things happen.'

'They are?'

'Firstly, that you do not need to think to make it happen because those positive thoughts are fixed in your mind that it becomes a natural state and secondly that the natural state is the certainty that creates the life you want to live because you knew that it was going to happen.'

'So, it takes will power?'

'Yes life is all about will power - for example if you want to be rich, you want to lose weight, you want to be your personal best then you have to have the will power to think the thoughts you need to think to make it happen, to ensure you believe that you are rich, that you have lost weight, that you are your personal best and the will power to take consistent action in line with your vision to make it happen.'

'Yes Fandango, now you have one last step to take.... **To free your mind from the perception prison.'**

'Do or do not, there is no try' - Yoda

Who has control you or your mind?
What will you choose?
What will you then will into your life?

A young wife fell sick and was about to die. 'I love you so much' she told her husband, 'I do not want to leave you. Do not go from me to any other woman, if you do, I will return as a ghost and cause you endless trouble.'

Soon the wife passed away. The husband respected her last wish for the first three months, but then he met another woman and fell in love with her. They became engaged to be married.

Immediately after the engagement a ghost appeared every night to the man, blaming him for not keeping his promise. The ghost was clever too. She told him what had transpired between himself and his new sweetheart. Whenever he gave his fiancée a present, the ghost would describe it in detail. She would even repeat conversations, and it so annoyed the man that he could not sleep. Someone advised him to take his problem to a Zen Master who lived close to the village. At length, in despair, the poor man went for help.

*'Your former wife became a ghost and knows everything you do' commented the master.
'Whatever you do or say, whatever you give your beloved, she knows. She must be a very wise ghost. Really you should admire such a ghost. The next time she appears, bargain with her. Tell her that she knows so much you can hide nothing from her, and that if she will answer you one question, you promise to break the engagement and remain single.'*

'What is the one question?' inquired the man.

The master replied 'Take a large handful of soy beans and ask her exactly how many beans you hold in your hand. If she cannot tell you, you will know she is only a figment of your imagination and will trouble you no longer.'

The next night, when the ghost appeared the man flattered her and told her that she knew everything.

'Indeed,' replied the ghost, 'and I know you went to see that Zen Master today.'

'And since you know so much,' demanded the man, 'tell me how many beans I hold in this hand!'

At that moment, the ghost disappeared and never returned.

THE MASTER

'Asking yourself these deeper questions opens up new ways of being in the world. It brings in a breath of fresh air. It makes life more joyful. The real trick to life is not to be in the know, but to be in the mystery.' - Fred Alan Wolf

Chapter 7 The Skyfire

We sit at the side of a vast lake reflecting the sky on fire with its array of colours scattered through the rainbow. Deep reds light up the sky with shades of orange, yellow, blue and green as the sky meets the landscape. Mountains surround the lake with tall trees guarding the fall of the sun, in this setting of pure ecstasy and delight that one feels kisses of life in the scenery that seems heaven sent. I sit with my Master in meditation staring out across this timeless landscape that fills me with tears of happiness. Upon the lake is a single boat with a single figure inside as I hear the gentle movement of the water across the lake.

'Look towards the boat on the lake, I want you to close your eyes and picture the figure in the boat and tell me who you see inside?'

'I see myself Master setting my own course across the lake, creating my own direction, at

peace with life and love. Gently moving with the flow of the lake in this vast water that holds all life.'

'And how do you feel?

'Placed before this infinite scene of beauty in happiness I cry tears of eternal sadness.'

'So, my young one we have come before all the heavenly glory what do you surmise?'

'Master, that life is a gift and we can choose to use it how we will. We can create our own landscape. We can create our own Skyfire. We can shape and change our own world. We can change our life and change our world.'

'What does the Skyfire represent?'

'I look at this magnificent landscape and although I do not understand life from a metaphysical point of view, I do understand that we should make the best use of the time given to us. The Skyfire represents our highest hope in all that we can be. For the human race can reach moments of divine inspiration for we all have vast amounts of potential and that is humanity's sorrow, as part of this essence and this realm, the soul's eventuality.

The sorrow that we don't understand life and that with all we create there will always be that we destroy. The cycle of life and death. We can choose the roles we want to play and the person we want to be. The piper at the gates of dawn, the child who has just been born, the angel searching for his wings, the lover who in ecstasy sings, the architect who creates his fate, the adventurer at the gate, the artist who awakes with a blank canvas, the wanderer and his shadow, the dreamer, the soul and the spirit, the essence and the realm.'

'So, Fandango how do we end?'

'As always with a new beginning, a new dawn for mankind, a new age of freedom.'

'Freedom from what?'

'Freedom from our own minds, not to be bound by the perception prison but to be free to create our own worlds.'

'What form of intelligence is that?'

'It is to have the fundamental intelligence and bedrock of who you are. This is your Psychological intelligence, the freedom to realise you have a choice about everything.

*The choice if you want to take it, make it or break it is that you do have that choice. I choose positive mental everything as my mindset for life, my map that I now choose to create, my own paradigm, my **own** life.'*

'Good my young apprentice, first we recognized IQ as our intelligence quotient with logical thinking the world's compass for our intelligence and how we should measure that through our mental intelligence. Our physical intelligence (PQ) is our spatial awareness in how we move and act in the world. Then came the revolution of emotional intelligence (EQ) that we have the freedom to choose our response in any given situation along with having emotional intelligence in life, and in our relationships, EQ is more important than our IQ. Then came Spiritual Intelligence (SQ) the freedom to choose one's own meaning, to have a cause, a purpose, a meaning for this life, for this soul. All are vitally important in creating the whole person that we should be mentally, physically, emotionally and spiritually balanced.

This in itself is a person of integrity and purpose but the fundamental intelligence, the bedrock of who you are is your psychological intelligence (PSYQ) and if you use that intelligence you can programme yourself to live the life you want to lead, to have the freedom to choose who you want to be when you want to be at any given time.'

'Yes, my Master I understand the seven noble truths...

*The **Brain** represented that we are conditioned in life by every experience that we become set in our ways and set in the way we respond to life. **The great thing is we have a choice to be who we want to be when we want to be, and we can challenge our conditioning.***

*The **Mirror** represented our self-awareness in that we need to be aware that we have been programmed so that we can review who we are, our values, our beliefs, our past conditioning, our past actions, and the positive and negative experiences that have shaped who we have become. **The ideal self is not an end goal but a way of life - a self one creates.***

*The **Cave** represented how our internal world creates our external world and how we are bound by fear by the countless chattering of our inner voice. By controlling that voice and* *creating the thoughts we want with positive self-talk we can shape the life we want. The world within creates the world without.* **Our perception has become our reality and we no longer need to be trapped within that perception prison, we are free to decide, free to choose, free to create the life, the person we want to be, the direction and more importantly our fate. And within our cave, our subterranean landscape of the mind lies all the wonder of the world.**

The **Wheel** *represented that we make our own luck through the right mindset in life.* **What you believe with a passion you will bring into your life***, it's as simple as that.* **Your expectations become your realities. It is my mental state that defines the moment and the meaning I apply to it. Nothing has any meaning other than the meaning I choose.**

The **Watchman** *represents how we should guard against negative thoughts entering our subconscious mind, our subterranean level to ensure that we create the life we want to live.* **There are three parts to programming, the vision of the ideal self, the secret of the law of attraction and the will power to sustain the positive thoughts and take positive action.**

*The **Will** represents will power. You create the life you want in your mind with 100% certainty that it will happen. **My will is to ensure the thoughts I make I then create in my life through the power of my will. The will to love is of the spirit. It is the will power to create the life we want to live, to sustain the vision of who we want to be. It is our will power that awakens in the morning and re-creates the landscape we desire to ensure that we are not left in the desert of lost souls and that we are not victims of our circumstances. It is through our will that we take consistent action.***

*The **Skyfire** is illumination and enlightenment that we say yes to life as a gift and make the most of each day. **We use our psychological intelligence to give us freedom from the perception prison to create the life we want to live and change the world the way we want it to be.**'*

'We have come far on this journey Fandango; you are now aware of the fire of your spirit and the depth of your soul what is next for you young one?'

'I realise that through meditation and a time of introspection that I can create the vision of who I want to be, the mission statement, the affirmations, the picture clear in my mind. I also realize that I now need to reflect on my past conditioning to ensure I act in line with my beliefs, my values and principles in line with my vision of my ideal self. I will build my self-esteem and self-concept by saying yes to life and yes to myself. In so doing I will be layering my mind to create the internal landscape that my subconscious will help to create in my external world.

I will then set goals in clear transparent steps with 100% certainty that they will happen, that they have already happened through which I will condition myself through positive affirmations 'I like myself', 'The world is conspiring to do me good', 'I am whole, perfect, powerful, strong, loving, harmonious and happy', 'I am fit and healthy', 'I earn £60,000', 'I live in a five bedroom house', and I will add feeling, pictures, and the benefits to me with each affirmation to make it real. Continually repeating over and over again to ensure I am reprogrammed with faith and belief in the creation of my ideal self - the Super You.

I will ensure through my will to love, my will power, that I awaken each morning and create the landscape I desire, and then take action in line with my vision, in line with my goals and affirmations. For it will be my will power that will ensure I continue to behave in line with my vision and values until my behaviour becomes a habit, and then I will challenge my behaviour again to set new levels of behaviour.

In essence, I will become all I can be and be all I can become.'

'I see and when will this happen?'

'It can only happen in one place my Master.'

'And where would that be?'

'In the present, for the only life we have is now. For the power that rings eternal, and the dreams that sing infinity, exist now in the present. It is being present that makes the difference in this life and through being present I create my own life instead of life creating me.'

'And where lies meaning in all of this?'

'There is fascination and inspiration in every moment, in all that I see, smell, touch, taste and feel. In all that I am in this present moment, in all that I become and be in this present moment. I create my own meaning in a life that was born of purpose as part of the pattern. The balance lies in my mental, physical, emotional, spiritual, and psychological conditioning and the power of life lies in the freedom to choose that conditioning.'

'And where lies the Skyfire?'

'The skyfire is one's moment of realisation in life, in one's awakening, in one's freedom from the perception prison. Enlightenment and illumination.'

'And so, Fandango what next?'

'In this moment, there is no next only definite conclusions and the inspiration in the setting of this sky on fire my Master.'

'Then let's close this chapter with the question of this moment who is the Master now?'

'The void is that which stands right in the middle of this and that.

---

*The void is all inclusive having no opposite - there is
nothing
Which it excludes or opposes. It is a living void,
because all forms come out of it and whoever realizes
the void is filled with life and power and the love of
all things.' - Bruce Lee*

What is your sky on fire?
What is your inspiration?
Who is your Master?

*A young and rather boastful champion challenged a
Zen master who was renowned for his skill as an
archer. The young man demonstrated remarkable
technical proficiency when he hit a distant bull's eye
on his first try, and then split that arrow with his
second shot. "There," he said to the old man, "see if
you can match that!" Undisturbed, the master did not
draw his bow, but rather motioned for the young
archer to follow him up the mountain. Curious about
the old fellow's intentions, the champion followed him
high into the mountain until they reached a deep
chasm spanned by a rather flimsy and shaky log.
Calmly stepping out onto the middle of the unsteady
and certainly perilous bridge, the old master picked a
far away tree as a target, drew his bow, and fired a
clean, direct hit. "Now it is your turn," he said as he
gracefully stepped back onto the safe ground. Staring
with terror into the seemingly bottomless and
beckoning abyss, the young man could not force
himself to step out onto the log, no less shoot at a
target. "You have much skill with your bow," the
master said, sensing his challenger's predicament,
"but you have little skill with the mind that lets loose
the shot."*

THE MASTER

Some asked master Yun-men: 'What is the eye of genuine teaching?' The master said, 'Everywhere!'
One-Word Zen

Epilogue: The Fool

Finally, we find ourselves within the clouds high above where all dreams begin and end with each tale in the making. Sat upon the clouds of dreams upon dreams in sweet illumination for I am free from the chains of the perception prison, no longer held down by the world, no longer conditioned by the external landscape. Free to become and free to be what I want to be.

This ending is the human races new beginning with a new dawn in the realization of one's true self, through soul and spirit with the essence and the realm for we can create our life.

'So, my Fandango, we sit upon the clouds of many shapes and faces looking down upon the world and in so doing looking in to your very soul because now the fundamental question now that you have this power is how you will choose to use it?'

'There are many paths my Master, paths that lead to disarray, paths that lead to destruction, paths that leads to joy, pleasure and contentment. What is for certain is that I can create my own path although there may be a few destinations along the way that find me. I shape my destiny and my destiny shapes me.'

'Looking upon the world what do you see?'

'I see those who choose to live a reactive life continuing to be controlled by their conditioning, bound to the perception prison and I see free souls moving to this new paradigm of psychological intelligence through the freedom of their choices.'

'And in looking into the world what do you see in your own heart and soul?'

'As mentioned nothing has any meaning other than the meaning that we give it but if I am to live my life in line with my ideal self through my visioning, the secret and the power of my will to love, and to be true to oneself then I will epitomize and share the love given to me. Not only do I choose the life of purpose given to me, but I create that purpose to make a

difference upon the greater subconscious and universal will of this world.'

'And how will you do that my young apprentice no more?'

'I will share my knowledge, I will share my love, and I will give of myself. I will spread this new word unto the people so that we can all choose the freedom of our choices and choose to be who we want to be when we want to be at any time, in any situation. And the world will re-awaken with awareness and accountability for this life, this world, this greater purpose to become all that we can be and be all that we can become. True meaning and purpose.'

'Is this not the fool's errand?'

'Ignorance is bliss they say but the will to love is heaven on earth for it is you, we and I together being our natural self.'

'But surely our purpose in life is to observe this universe, this life and simply be for the universe would exist not if there was no observer to observe that it exists?'

'Master what if the universe is here because we have created it and actually the universe will always be as long as we continue to create through our thoughts and through our actions.'

'Perhaps Fandango, perhaps....and with every cloud there is a silver lining.'

'I remember as a child I could see all kinds of shapes, animals, places and faces in the clouds and that I always looked to the sky when lost in thought thinking of my dreams.'

'And what happened to your dreams?'

'I awake every morning and the dream begins my Master....'

'I see, then the last lesson is upon us look now at the mirror in the clouds and what do you see?'

'I see everything.'

'And?'

'I see you.'

'And who am I?'

'You are me.'

During a momentous battle, a Japanese general decided to attack even though his army was greatly outnumbered. He was confident they would win, but his men were filled with doubt. On the way to the battle, they stopped at a religious shrine. After praying with the men, the general took out a coin and said, "I shall now toss this coin. If it is heads, we shall win. If tails, we shall lose. Destiny will now reveal itself."

He threw the coin into the air and all watched intently as it landed. It was heads. The soldiers were so overjoyed and filled with confidence that they vigorously attacked the enemy and were victorious. After the battle, a lieutenant remarked to the general, "No one can change destiny."

"Quite right," the general replied as he showed the lieutenant the coin, which had heads on both sides.

Never give up on your dreams
Never ever give in
For the sky can be your home
And your dreams can be your reality

You are your own Master

THE MASTER
A Journey of Meaning and Purpose

What do you really know?
What do your senses tell you?
Where do you really live?

Who do you want to be?
What do you want?
Where are you going?

When you look at yourself in the mirror who are you?
How have you been conditioned by life?
How can you re-condition the landscape of your mind?

What is your cave filled with?
How can you free your mind?
How can you create your life?

Are you victim of fate or do you make your own luck?
What is your mental state and mindset?
Do you take risks or play safe?

What thoughts are you being conditioned by?
How can you change your thinking?
What do you want in your life?

Who has control you or your mind?
What will you choose?
What will you then will into your life?

What is your sky on fire?
What is your inspiration?
Who is your Master?

Carefully watch your THOUGHTS,
for they become your WORDS.
Manage and watch your WORDS,
for they become your ACTIONS
Consider and judge your ACTIONS,
for they become your HABITS,
Acknowledge and watch your HABITS,
for they shall become your VALUES.
Understand and embrace your
VALUES,
for they become your destiny.

\- Mahatma Gandhi

Mindset Services

Paul Corke – Keynote Speaking & Facilitation
Paul is a Founder, Author, Leadership Thinker, Facilitator, and Speaker whose talks are interactive, provocative, and engaging, to inspire leaders to think different.

Paul was a very fortunate survivor of the Hillsborough Football Disaster in 1989, which shaped his mindset at an early age, and for the last 30 years he has researched mindset, success and happiness. From this, Paul has developed his theory of psychological intelligence, which is about how we can all be the best version of ourselves. His talks about 'The Mindset Equation', are used as the vehicle to describe the secret to success.

Paul is also passionate about leadership and can provide insight into how leadership will evolve in the future, and how to build an effective leadership culture. As we know, with the onset of exponential, technological and digital change, it is essential for leaders to demonstrate resilience and agility to the demanding forces at play in work.

Paul also talks about a leader's mindset, and how a shift is required to demonstrate key leadership success factors to thrive and survive in the ever-changing landscape of work. He also provides bespoke talks on key leadership subjects to tailor the content to your organisation.

Paul has previously spent 25 years plus developing leaders in the corporate world through a range of different approaches, to provide a responsive, experiential, collaborative, and innovative approach to Leadership Development. In addition, he provides facilitation of leadership conferences and events, to ensure they are engaging, and the key leadership messages are delivered. Paul now owns his own successful leadership consultancy called, 'Leadership Architecture', defining leadership for organisations, along with providing appropriate leadership architecture and solutions to drive organisational effectiveness and profitability.

Paul Corke's Master Mindset Groups

Paul's 'Master Mindset' Groups are self, leadership, and business development networking groups. Using the content from his books, Paul facilitates Master Mindset Groups, to deliver powerful lessons.

In the group, you will focus on developing your mindset to be the best version of you, develop your leadership skills, and also apply the lessons to building your new or existing business. Groups of 12-16 individuals come together to have a unique mindset learning and development experience, whilst at the same time, the opportunity to network with like-minded people and leaders.

Paul facilitates face-to-face and virtual open groups for individuals and businesses. He also uses the approach to work within organisations to bring leaders from across the business together to develop, grow and develop their business culture. Paul also runs cross-organisational groups, bringing leaders from different sectors and backgrounds to learn, develop, and share experiences.

Paul Corke Mindset Coaching
If you are looking for a premium coaching service to develop your mindset, Paul will provide coaching based on the content of his books. Paul has a Masters in Executive Coaching as well as ILM 7 in Coaching and Mentoring, is an accredited coach and has over 25 years' coaching experience working in large organisations, and as a life mindset coach.

Paul's Leadership Consultancy – Leadership Architecture
Leadership Architecture provide leadership consultancy to enhance your organisational effectiveness, and build leadership capability to create your desired culture, increase company performance, and maximise profitability. This is possible by defining leadership for your organisation, providing the appropriate leadership architecture and solutions, to build exceptional leadership capability.

Paul also provides Executive and Leadership Coaching for clients, to develop leadership thinking, capability and enhance performance. Coaching enables leadership effectiveness to the benefit of the coach and the organisation.

Mindset Equation Individual, Team and Organisational Report

As part of Paul's consultancy work, and using the content from The Mindset Equation, Paul has developed a leading psychometric Mindset Equation Questionnaire. The questionnaire provides an in-depth assessment of an individual's mindset and a report is generated to develop self-awareness. This allows an individual to reflect on their mindset strengths and development areas enabling effective coaching using the report.

The tool provides different levels of assessment: 1. Self-assessment, 2. Team assessment, 3. Organisational mindset assessment. This is a unique and leading tool in its field. For organisations looking to develop their employees and leader's mindset, this tool, used in conjunction with your leadership development and business strategy, provides a very effective way to build the culture you desire and maximise the profitability of your organisation.

All enquiries on the services above please contact:
info@leadershiparchitect.co.uk

Printed in Poland
by Amazon Fulfillment
Poland Sp. z o.o., Wrocław

49809665R00065